Liberation
Summer

By Stewart Mitchell

This book is dedicated to my two children, Taj and Nazir Mitchell. May you find your passion in life and become the greatest at what your creative minds allow you to be. Live your dreams, protect the vulnerable, and always love each other.

Liberate your mind. Liberate animals. Liberate humanity.

Chapter one

Rude Awakening

Brownsville, Brooklyn, N.Y.
June 28, 7:01 a.m.

Early in the morning, Jayden Young was awoken by the ringing of the alarm on his smartphone. "It's way too early," he thought and decided to hit snooze. A few minutes went by, and he was startled by his mother's knocking on his bedroom door.

"Hey, Jayden! Get up. It's the last day of school!" she yelled. "I have to talk to you before you leave." Jayden groaned in response and sat up on the edge of the bed to collect his thoughts.

After he finished showering and got dressed for school, Jayden went to the kitchen, where his mother, Ms. Young, was preparing breakfast for him and his 5-year-old sister, Tara. "Hey, Ma. You wanted to talk to me?" he asked.

"Yeah, Jay. Sit down," she replied. Jayden took a seat as his mother put food on the table. She had made scrambled eggs, sausage, and pancakes, with a side of orange juice. As they ate, Ms. Young looked at him and remarked, "Jay, today is your last day of school. You're going to start college in a few months, but in between now and then, you have to get a job."

Jayden looked startled. "A job? C'mon, Ma! That's going to ruin my whole summer!" He felt frustrated.

Ms. Young looked Jayden in the eye and calmly tried to explain why he had to work. "Jay, you're getting older. I'm sorry you feel like this will ruin your summer plans, but you'll be 18 later this year, and you have to learn how to take care of yourself, baby." She gently grabbed his hand. He slumped back in his chair and rolled his eyes in annoyance.

"You're a young adult. You have to learn how to be responsible," Ms. Young explained. "It's getting harder to take care of you and your sister on the money I'm making, and college tuition is very expensive, so this will definitely help me out as well."

Jayden sat up and quietly picked at his food while his sister looked on, not knowing what to make of it all. Ms. Young looked at Jayden, waiting for a response. "All right, Ma," he said reluctantly, with a forced smile. "I hear what you're saying. You're right."

Ms. Young smiled. "I know you're upset, but I would appreciate it so much."

The Young family sat and finished their breakfast before heading off to their destinations. Ms. Young would take Tara to daycare and then head off to her job at the airport. Jayden left for school. He wore his favorite royal blue baseball cap, his royal blue tracksuit, which fit nicely on his slim athletic frame, and also a matching pair of leather Air Wavy sneakers. Off he went to say goodbye to his teachers and friends on his last day of high school.

Right in front of the school stood a couple of boys loudly talking together. The tallest among them was Tristan. He looked over his shoulder and saw Jayden coming up the block. "Yo, Jay! Whattup?!" He was noisy and animated. The other boys also looked up to see Jayden striding toward them.

"What's up, Tristan!" Jayden had a big smile. They greeted each other with a fist bump and a hug. He greeted the other boys with fist bumps and high fives.

Tristan threw his arm around Jayden's shoulders in excitement. "Yo, last day of school, kid!" he exclaimed. "Summer is about to be lit!" Jayden rolled his eyes, remembering what his mother had made him agree to. "Hey, Jay, what's good, bro?" Tristan asked, concerned. "Why do you look so down?"

Jayden looked up at Tristan. "I'm probably gonna be busy all summer, man."

"Bro, what are you talking about?" Tristan asked incredulously. "I just got my license. I convinced my mom that she should let me use the car now since she takes the train to work and school is over." He tapped Jayden on the chest and said enthusiastically, "We're going to Virginia Beach, we gonna check out the party scene down at the Jersey Shore, we're going to Philly for cheesesteak ... yo, kid, we gonna be all over!"

Jayden shook his head. "Nah, man. My mother told me I have to look for a job."

"Oh, no! Your mom is making you get a job?" Tristan asked. "Bro, you gonna miss out on all the fun! I had so much planned for us!" Tristan was just as disappointed as Jayden. "I know you're going to college to major in business, but we have some *major business* to address this summer, baby!" That got a little chuckle out of Jayden. Tristan was outgoing and adventurous, but he was also very understanding and open-minded. He was the type of guy who would listen to your problems and try to help. And he was loyal.

"I guess you gotta do what you gotta do, kid." He sighed. "Ya mom is counting on you—that's more important than partying all summer." At the end of the school day, almost everyone hung around for a while. They wanted to take selfies with their friends and favorite teachers. Jayden, along with everyone else, gave his final hugs and bid farewell and good luck to all. It was an emotional moment, because everyone was moving on to the next phase of their lives. School was officially over, and summer had officially started.

Chapter Two

Reporting for Duty

Downtown Brooklyn, N.Y.
July 2, 9 a.m.

After Jayden's graduation ceremony, he started filling out applications online for various jobs. He received a call from a fried chicken restaurant called New Orleans Roasters, one specifically located in Downtown Brooklyn. The establishment was popular, with no fewer than 20 locations in Brooklyn alone. Jayden and his friends often ate there. The store manager, Mr. Brown, called him in for an interview. Decked out in a white dress shirt, navy blue khakis, and black leather loafers, Jayden had high hopes.

Jayden sat and spoke with Mr. Brown for a few minutes, and the manager was impressed with his poise and the way he answered questions. Jayden had charisma, and he had developed speaking skills on the debate team at school. Mr. Brown offered him a job working evenings at the restaurant. He accepted, got his work schedule, shook hands with Mr. Brown, thanked him, and left. On his way home, he took out his smartphone and called his mother to tell her he had landed a job.

"That's good news, baby!" she said excitedly. "I'm so proud of you. You're becoming a man, Jayden. Now you'll have to learn how to manage your money, OK? You can't spend all of it on Air Wavy sneakers and smartphones," she joked. "You'll have to open a bank account and save money for your college books."

On his way home, Jayden bumped into Tristan. "What's up, Jay? Where are you going with that shirt and them shoes, bro?"

Jayden replied, "I just came from a job interview downtown at New Orleans Roasters. I'll be starting there after the Fourth of July."

"Yo, that's cool, man! At least you'll still be free for the annual July 4th barbecue and block party. Don't want to miss Mr. Louis' famous barbecue!" Tristan rubbed his hands together and smacked his lips. "Man, I can taste those ribs and burgers already!" Jayden laughed at his animated friend's body language. Tristan added, "It still sucks that you won't be able to hang out this summer, but at least you'll be making your own money. You don't have to ask your mother anymore."

"Yeah, whatever," Jayden said, half-heartedly. He still wasn't thrilled with the idea of working all summer. He was only 17 and still wanted to hang out with his friends and enjoy his summer vacation before college started at the end of September.

As they walked, they chatted about sports, girls, and their favorite topic—sneakers! Tristan asked Jayden enthusiastically, "Did you see Air Wavy just released a new color to the Wavy 5's on their website?"

Jayden was excited to hear this. He took out his phone to see what they looked like. "These are dope!" Jayden grinned.

Tristan added, "Yeah, I like how the red leather goes with the white suede. They'll be out at the end of the month, and you'll be able to get a pair before everybody else, since you're gonna be working!"

Jayden thought about it. "Yeah, maybe working for my own money won't be so bad after all!" They both laughed then went their separate ways.

A few days later, Jayden reported for work. It was his first night, so he would be trained by Felipe, the night shift manager. Felipe was 25 and had already been working at New Orleans Roasters for three years. He was very ambitious and had worked his way up from a part-time restaurant closer to a full-time shift manager. He wanted to become a district manager one day, overseeing multiple stores. He introduced Jayden to the rest of the crew.

There were two cashiers, Janet and Iesha, and two cooks, Mike and Stan. They all welcomed Jayden with a smile and good wishes. "Jayden, since you're new, you'll be in charge of making sure the kitchen gets cleaned every night and that food is prepped for the cooks to fry and roast," said Felipe. "I don't want to throw you to the wolves just yet by putting you on the register. Customers can be a handful sometimes!" he chuckled. Jayden nodded, smiled, and followed his lead.

Jayden was a fast learner. Every night, he had to unload the delivery truck and place the items in the restaurant cooler. He would then take boxes of chicken parts that contained 100 breasts, legs, wings, and thighs and prepare them.

That meant that he had to clean and batter the chicken so the cooks could start frying it. Some boxes contained chicken parts that were seasoned with the stores' special recipe so the cooks could roast them in the oven. After the kitchen closed, normally at 9 p.m., Jayden and one of the cooks would clean and sanitize the cooking equipment and the dishes for the next morning. Every night, Jayden was allowed to take home a boxed dinner that consisted of any two pieces of chicken and any two side dishes, plus a dinner roll. Since he liked the fried chicken at the restaurant, he didn't mind the free meal at all!

After working at the restaurant for a week, Jayden was used to the routine and liked working with his crew. Even though he would be missing his friends for most of the summer, he made some new ones at work. He realized that his new companions made a tough job seem a little bit easier.

Back at home, in the morning, Jayden and Tara sat down to eat breakfast at the kitchen table. Their mother made their breakfast of cheese omelets, bacon strips, home fries, and orange juice. She sat down at the table to eat with her kids.

"So, Jayden, you haven't told me about the job," she said. "How's it going? Do you like it?"

Jayden shrugged his shoulders and replied, "Yeah, it's OK. The staff is cool. Some days are busy, and some days it's just steady."

Tara teased her big brother, "You just like the job because they give you free chicken!" Everyone laughed.

Ms. Young asked, "What are you doing up so early today? Now that you're working, I notice that you usually sleep a lot later, and I don't see you when you get home."

Between bites, Jayden replied, "I have the day off, so I'll go to the bank and open an account to deposit my first paycheck."

Ms. Young smiled, proud of her son. "I'm so glad to see you taking your job so seriously." He smiled back, and they chatted some more while they finished eating.

Chapter Three

Air Wavy

Downtown Brooklyn, N.Y.
July 30, 8 a.m.

A few weeks had gone by. Jayden had been working steady hours at his job. He had been collecting paychecks and always deposited the funds into his bank account. The evening crew at work split the tips they were getting. He had saved up more than enough money in tips alone to buy the new Air Wavy sneakers.

Saturday morning, Jayden got in line outside the popular sneaker store Athletic Footwear. Jayden knew that the line of people waiting to get in would be long, so he got to the store early in the morning. He was one of the first people in line, so this almost guaranteed he would get the sneakers he wanted in his size. The line of people stretched down Fulton Street, where Athletic Footwear was located, to the end of the block and around the corner.

Everyone was excited about the release of these new sneakers, especially Jayden. Once the doors to Athletic Footwear opened, the workers started letting customers inside three at a time. Jayden was sixth in line, so he waited patiently for the first group to make their purchases. It was his turn next. He greeted one of the salespeople with a smile.

"Lemme get a pair of those new Wavy 5s in a size 9, please," he said. A few seconds later, the employee came out of the storage room in the back with a black-and-silver box. He opened it up so Jayden could see the sneakers.

"Yo, boss, are these good? You want to try 'em on?" the salesperson asked.
Jayden's eyes were locked on the sneakers in the box and, grinning from ear to ear, he replied: "Nah, I'm good, man. I'll take 'em!" He was thinking to himself how great the sneakers looked close up.

Jayden approached the checkout counter. Two hundred dollars later, he was the proud owner of a brand-new pair of red-and-white Air Wavy 5s.

Later that afternoon, he went to work ready for his shift, when Felipe called him to the back of the store for a brief meeting in the manager's office. Mr. Brown was sitting in front of his computer, going over sales and orders. He stood up to shake Jayden's hand. "Jayden! How are you doing?" he asked with a big smile.

Jayden gave him a firm handshake, smiled back, and said, "I'm doing well, Mr. Brown. Thanks for asking."

Mr. Brown sat back down. "I hear nothing but good things about you. Keep it up! There is always room for advancement in this company."

Jayden smiled. "Thank you, sir."

"Someday you might be running your own restaurant and giving out orders instead of taking them!" Mr. Brown joked and he and Felipe laughed. "Felipe here is one of a few people up for promotion. In about eight weeks, there's going to be a grand opening of another restaurant in Brownsville, and I think he would do a stellar job of running that location." Jayden knew of the location—it was just a few blocks from his own home. Mr. Brown gestured at Felipe. "I pushed hard for this young man to run that store as the head manager." Felipe beamed with pride.

Finally, Mr. Brown got down to business. "Jayden, you know the new sale starts tomorrow. We're going to have a special in-restaurant sale on buckets of fried chicken. Would you be able to work an extra 16 hours next week? We're expecting double the business we normally see. More hours equals more money in your pocket, young man." Mr. Brown assured him. "If you do what's best for the business, you'll start to be considered for promotions."

Felipe chimed in. "Yeah, Jayden, look where it's got me! In a few years, you could be making the big bucks as a manager, too!"

Jayden thought about it for a second then agreed. He figured that his summer was already ruined by the fact that he had to work, so he might as well make the extra cash. He shook Mr. Brown's hand and agreed to work the extra hours.

Mr. Brown was pleased with Jayden's answer and said, "Thank you so much! I appreciate it. Now remember, it's going to be busy! Double the workload, so I hope you're ready for it!"

Chapter Four

Chickens Equals Dollars

Downtown Brooklyn, N.Y.
August 1, 1 p.m.

As he had promised, Jayden showed up to work earlier than his usual time of 4 p.m. and as Mr. Brown had promised, it was busy! The delivery truck came early, so Jayden got right to work, unloading and preparing the chicken parts for the cooks. Felipe was frantically trying to keep the customers happy and making sure everyone was working safely and efficiently.

"Jayden, keep those chickens coming!" he yelled from the counter. Jayden was working at a fast pace. He was cleaning, seasoning, and battering what seemed like an endless stream of whole chickens and chicken parts. While he was used to handling 10 to 15 boxes of chicken parts, he was trying to meet the increased demands of the night. He had 35 boxes of chicken parts that he had to prepare for the cooks —more than double the normal amount! The customers were becoming more demanding, the cooks were frying and roasting as fast as they could, and the cashiers were briskly ringing up customers' nonstop orders!

In the midst of cleaning and preparing the chicken parts, Jayden started to feel a little overwhelmed with the job he was doing that day. The more frustrated he became, the more arduous the work became. He began to wonder how it was possible for so much chicken to be so readily available. How was it possible to have so many chickens delivered to the store at one time? Then it occurred to him that there were other New Orleans Roasters getting the same delivery. How could a farm supply tens of thousands of chickens to every single store on a daily basis and never run out?

At the end of what turned out to be a very long, tough day, Jayden and a cook named Mike, who had been working all day, too, left the restaurant together and walked toward the train station. "I'm so tired, man," said Mike.

Jayden, still curious about the chicken, asked, "Where do you think all that chicken comes from?"

Mike shrugged. "I don't know. I never thought about it.

"But don't you find it strange that we never run out of chickens to cook?" Jayden asked him, perplexed.

He laughed. "No, and I don't want to see another chicken for the rest of the night!" They boarded the train for home.

After a week of working long hours in the same hectic conditions, Jayden was mentally and physically exhausted. Dealing with pressure from Felipe to work faster and putting up with impatient customers with bad attitudes, Jayden's thoughts were still on the endless stream of chickens and where it was coming from. Day after day, it just seemed like an unlimited number of chickens were arriving at the store to be cooked. It just seemed almost surreal, and he started to wonder why he hadn't noticed this sooner.

He also started to notice how queasy his stomach felt after eating the fried chicken meals every night. He loved the taste of the free meals he was given to take home, but they were making him sick, and he noticed that he had also added a few unwanted pounds to his slim frame. He wondered, if the food was making him gain unhealthy weight and making his stomach uncomfortable, was it having the same effect on the daily customers?

The next Saturday, Jayden showed up for work as normal. Felipe held a little group huddle with the evening crew. He was holding a report of the prior week's sales.

"Hey, listen up, guys!" he exclaimed. "I want to thank all of you for last week. We exceeded expectations with the mid-summer sale!" Everyone applauded. "We outsold every other restaurant in the district, and we're ahead of our projected sales for the quarter!" Felipe said. He went on to say a few more words of encouragement to the crew before sending everyone off to work. Jayden went to his work station, where he began cleaning and battering chicken parts. Felipe passed by on his way to check the temperature of the coolers.

Jayden stopped for a moment and turned to his supervisor. "Hey Felipe, did you ever stop and wonder why we never run out of chickens to sell?"

"No, they don't pay me to think about that. They pay me to make sure the chicken gets sold and the customers are happy." Felipe continued checking the coolers. Jayden gazed at the floor and thought about Felipe's answer. He wondered why he cared but no one else did.

"Jayden, come on. Get your head in the game," Felipe said, trying to snap Jayden out of his deep thoughts. "The cooks are going to need another round of chickens!" he added. Jayden got back to work.

After a few more hours, Jayden's shift was over, and he got ready to leave. Mike had already set aside a meal for him. Jayden took the meal despite what it seemed to be doing to his health. Curiosity was getting the better of him, though. On his way out of the restaurant, he walked past the empty chicken boxes that were left on the sidewalk for recycling. He took out his phone and snapped a picture of one of the boxes that had the name of the farm where the chickens were raised. He was careful to get the name and number so he could contact them. He realized he was starting to become obsessed with learning how the chickens were farmed and raised. He still couldn't understand how so many chickens could be raised for food so fast.

Chapter Five

Another Rude Awakening

Brownsville, Brooklyn, N.Y.
August 10, 10:30 a.m.

About a week later, Jayden finally called the farm in Pennsylvania that supplied the chickens. He sat at the kitchen table and ate a small breakfast that he had prepared for himself – ham, fried eggs, hash browns, and a cup of fruit juice. After dialing the number that he had gotten off the box at work, he was put on hold for a few minutes. Finally someone answered the phone and said: "Riverside Farms. This is Janet speaking. How can I assist you?"

"Hi. My name is Jayden Young," he stated. "I work at a New Orleans Roasters here in Brooklyn, where you make deliveries."

"Hello, Mr. Young. How can I assist you today?" asked Janet.

"I was a little curious as to how fast your chickens grow," Jayden began.

"I'm not sure that I understand your question, Mr. Young," Janet responded.

"Well, it seems like we never run out of chickens at work, and I wanted to know just how often the chickens are bred to meet the needs of every restaurant you service," Jayden clarified.

"Well, our chickens are fed a healthy diet of grains such as corn, and they are free-range, and we have a specialist that oversees the production process," Janet explained.

"Would it be possible to take a tour of the farm to see the process in person?" Jayden inquired.

"Well, it's a tedious process to visit due to health codes," Janet responded. "Might I suggest a viral visit on our website or checking out the footage our company uploads to WebVideos?"

"Well ..." Jayden stopped mid-sentence, realizing he wasn't going to get the answer he was looking for. "OK, thank you for your time, Janet. Have a good day," he said instead.

"Yes, you, too, Mr. Young."

Jayden ended the call and finished his meal. With a few hours to spare before he started his shift at the restaurant, Jayden decided to look for videos about raising chickens on the social media site WebVideos. He sat on the couch looking at his phone and watched a few videos posted by Riverside Farms and other farms that raise chickens.

After a few minutes, he came across a video posted by an animal rights group called LIFE, which stood for Liberation Is for Everyone. The video was titled, "The Truth About Factory Farming," which piqued Jayden's curiosity— maybe he would get a different point of view.

The video showed the hidden truth of what really happens to animals on farms, as opposed to the other videos, produced by the farms' public relations teams, which only show the viewer what they want them to see. The video Jayden was watching was undercover footage of chickens living in very cramped, uncomfortable conditions crammed together by the tens of thousands. He saw chickens' beaks being cut with blades so they wouldn't peck each other to death.

He listened as the narrator described how the chickens were fed antibiotics, causing them to grow larger than normal in much less time. They grew so large that they weren't able to support their own bodyweight because of the unnatural way they were being fed and raised, and many collapsed. Farmers walked nonchalantly down the aisles of cages stuffed with chickens, yanking them out like they were inanimate objects.

Jayden also saw videos of pigs and cows being beaten and forcibly impregnated for mass production of meat and dairy. They, too, lived in miserable conditions. He couldn't believe his eyes. He saw farm workers slamming piglets into the concrete floor! He started to feel guilty about his enjoyment of bacon, ham, eggs, and chicken.

Jayden listened as the narrator explained how the consumer was indirectly contributing to these animals' poor treatment. As long as there was a demand for meat, eggs, and dairy, these practices would continue.

With his eyes glued to his phone, Jayden started to question everything he had been taught about animals on farms. The animated images of happy cows and pigs he was used to seeing on cartons of milk and packaged meat products suddenly seemed hypocritical. As more graphic images flashed across the screen, the narrator in the video spoke about other aspects of the inhumane treatment that these innocent animals endure and about their short life span because they are killed at a very young age. Jayden was finally getting the answer to his question, but it wasn't what he had expected: Animals were being treated like inanimate objects—mass-produced to meet the consumer demand for meat.

After watching a few more minutes of the agonizing footage, Jayden searched for the LIFE website. He wanted to learn more about their cause. As he read through their website, he discovered that the organization was very passionate about animal liberation. He wondered why he had never heard of this organization before and why he never saw animals as sentient beings before watching the LIFE videos.

The further he looked into it, the deeper his realization that animal cruelty wasn't confined to the food industry—it was taking place in almost every aspect of life. His perspective on animals started to change.

Chapter Six

Where Is the Compassion?

Downtown Brooklyn, N.Y.
August 10, 3 p.m.

Shortly after watching the videos on animal cruelty, Jayden showed up for his shift at the restaurant. He was still in shock from what he had seen and was trying to process the information while also attending to his job duties. He was starting to see the connection between the helpless, innocent animals and the horrific process they underwent to become a meal on someone's dinner table.

Mike came into the prep area where Jayden was seasoning the chicken pieces. He took a tray of chicken that Jayden had already prepared.

"Hey, Mike, you ever think about how this chicken we're serving to customers was once a living being?" Jayden asked.

Mike rolled his eyes. "Jayden, what's with you and these questions about chicken all of a sudden?" He picked up the tray and headed back toward the kitchen. "Bro, I don't know, and I don't really care, to be honest," he said as he walked away.

Later that evening, Felipe walked into the preparation room doing his usual temperature check. Jayden paused for a second then asked him, "Felipe, have you ever seen a factory-farm video?"

"Yeah, I've seen a few," he answered, while checking the coolers.

"How do you feel about them?" asked Jayden. "I mean, isn't it crazy that farmers kill these animals that did nothing to us, just for money?"

Felipe looked at Jayden. "Yeah, I agree it's terrible, but that's the cycle of life, kid. This is how we survive. We eat other animals. We dominate the food chain!" He seemed proud that humans are so powerful.

"It seems unnecessary to me," Jayden mumbled.

"It's not unnecessary when you have a family to feed," said Felipe. "What's gotten into you lately, Jay? This is how we make our money and keep food on the table." He headed back toward the front of the restaurant. "Get back to work! Keep those chickens coming!"

Hours later, Jayden's shift was over and he was headed home. Mike called out to him from the kitchen area. "Yo, Jay, don't forget your meal! I left a box for you in the warmer!"

Jayden, his face buried in his phone watching more LIFE videos, replied, "I'm good. I'mma skip the meal tonight ... thanks." Mike was surprised. He knew how much Jayden enjoyed the chicken dinners because he took one every night.

Jayden continued watching videos on his phone as he walked to the subway. He was educating himself on animal agriculture and the ways it affects not just the direct victims—the animals— but also the people who eat animal products. He also learned that restaurants like New Orleans Roasters and other fast-food chains have a negative impact on consumer health. He always noticed how slow and heavy he felt after eating the chicken dinners from the restaurant. The unwanted pounds that he had gained were more proof of what he was reading. Unhealthy weight gain could lead to obesity and other serious health problems. He learned that a huge reason why almost 700,000 Americans die of heart disease is their consumption of meat, dairy, and fast food. He thought about his neighborhood and what types of businesses flourished there. The statistics started to add up. The fast food that caused illnesses like heart disease mainly affected poor communities, and Jayden's neighborhood was jam-packed with many different fast-food restaurants. The information both angered and saddened him. Not only were animals being horribly affected by the restaurants and by the agriculture industry, his neighborhood was being negatively affected, too.

Chapter Seven

Family Values

Brownsville, Brooklyn, N.Y.
August 12, 9 a.m.

It was Saturday morning, and Ms. Young was in the kitchen preparing breakfast for herself and Tara. Jayden was usually asleep at this time, but today he was awake in his room, scrolling through websites about veganism on his laptop to find out more about ditching animal products. Ever since he had questioned the mass production of chickens for food, he had become obsessed with the way animals are treated by humans.

He started to become interested in going vegan. The realization that animals are mistreated by humans and exploited for profit had Jayden questioning everything he was taught about them. "I can't believe I was contributing to their suffering all this time," he said to himself. On the LIFE website, he read articles about animals who are not only farmed and slaughtered but also abused in circuses. He thought back to his enjoyment of the circus when he was younger. He also read articles about companies that test household and personal care products on animals. He started to realize how many different items his family uses on a daily basis that were made by companies that test their products on animals. After watching so many videos and reading so many articles about animal cruelty, he knew he didn't want to eat anything that was made from animals ever again, so he also searched the internet for vegan foods and recipes.

Jayden sat on the edge of his bed deep in thought. Glancing across the room, he looked at the new pair of Air Wavy sneakers he bought a few weeks ago. He remembered how excited he was to purchase them on their release date. He recalled how much attention he got whenever he wore them.

He thought about the LIFE video he had watched concerning the leather and fur industries and the fact that some animals were raised and killed just for their skin. He had always thought that he had nice taste in fashion—until now. Now he realized that not only did the trendy sneakers cost him $200, they also cost an animal's life. Jayden walked over to his closet and started shuffling through all the clothes on the rack and on the shelves. Realizing that many of his favorite

garments were made from the skins of animals, he shook his head in shame. One by one, he went through each item. His favorite fall jacket was genuine leather, his favorite blue baseball cap was made from a wool blend, a winter coat with goose down was hung in the back of the closet, and he owned a few old pairs of Air Wavy sneakers that were made from leather as well.

Jayden entered the kitchen, where his mother and Tara were sitting at the table eating breakfast. "Good morning, baby!" Ms. Young said. "I didn't know you were up. Do you want breakfast?"

"No thanks, Ma. I'm good." He reached up into the cabinet and took down a box of oatmeal and a banana off the counter. He looked over and smiled at his little sister. "Are you staying out of trouble?" he asked her playfully. Tara responded by sticking her tongue out and giggling at her big brother. Jayden filled a small pot with water so he could boil the oatmeal.

Ms. Young was surprised. "Jayden, I thought you weren't hungry."
"I'm just in the mood for some oatmeal today, Ma."
"You're not gonna have any ham and eggs sunny side up?" asked Ms. Young. "I'm surprised, because that's your favorite."

Jayden sat down at the table with his mother while the water on the stove was heating up. "Ma, did you ever think about how we get our food?"

Ms. Young looked puzzled but answered, "We get it from the supermarket. Are you OK, Jay?" Tara laughed, and Ms. Young laughed along with her.

"Ma, I'm serious." Jayden had a hint of frustration in his voice. "Did you ever think about what happens to these animals before we eat them?"

Ms. Young paused and then responded, "No, I never thought about it. It's just the cycle of life.

That's their purpose, Jay. That's why they're put here."

"You think unnecessarily killing an animal to eat their flesh is their purpose?" he asked.
That comment caught Tara's attention. She looked up from her plate and asked curiously, "The animal died? Who killed the animal?"
Ms. Young quickly turned to Tara. "No, no, baby. Nobody killed an animal." Then she turned back to Jayden, and said, "Don't say things like that in front of your sister!"
"Why should we hide the truth from her?" asked Jayden, "She should know where her food comes from. Everybody should know!"

"Tara, go play in your room," Ms. Young instructed her young daughter. "Jayden, what's gotten into you? Why are you talking like this?"

Jayden stood up to turn off the stove and mix his oatmeal into the boiling water. "I've been doing some reading, and I just realize how mistreated

animals are for the sake of our own benefit," he told his mother.

"They're not mistreated, Jayden. The animals hardly know what's going on. The animals don't feel pain. They don't have feelings like us."

Jayden was cutting the banana to put in his oatmeal when he stopped and turned around. "Ma, you don't think the animals have feelings?" he asked in shock. "They're fully conscious of what happens to them. They have the same senses we do."

"So does this mean you won't eat meat anymore, Jay?" asked Ms. Young. "I think you should talk to our family doctor before making that decision. That doesn't sound healthy. There are bigger issues to worry about than animals."

"Yes, I'm going to stop eating meat, and I think you and Tara should, too, at least for your health if for nothing else," said Jayden. He turned back around to mix the bananas into his oatmeal.

"Jayden there's nothing wrong with eating meat," Ms. Young scolded as she cleared the table. "I was raised on it, and so were your grandparents."

Jayden shot back, "Why do you think grandpa has heart disease, Ma? This food is killing us!"

This angered Ms. Young. "Jayden, watch what comes out of your mouth! Don't talk about your grandfather like that! I don't know what's gotten into you, but I'm done having this conversation." She put the dishes in the sink.

"I didn't mean any disrespect, Ma," said Jayden. "I just think we could be making better choices, that's all."

Chapter Eight

Over It

Downtown Brooklyn, N.Y.
August 14, 5:10 p.m.

An hour into his shift at the restaurant, Jayden was hustling, trying to satisfy the cooks' demand for chicken parts. He was cleaning and battering box after box of chicken. He kept thinking about the videos of animals getting tortured and that he was part of the problem.

Subconsciously, he started to slow down on chicken preparation, and the cooks began complaining. "Jay, we need more chickens! C'mon, bro!" Mike yelled into the prep area.

"All right, I got you!" Jayden yelled back. Over the last few weeks, Jayden's perception of his job had changed. He no longer looked at the chicken parts as food. What he saw was animals who had died so that human beings could enjoy the taste of their flesh for a 10-minute meal.

Not only did Jayden recognize the unnecessary suffering that the animals had endured, he also started to notice what kind of foods the people in his community were eating and that in his neighborhood, there were no health food stores or farmers' markets. But there was no shortage of

burger and chicken franchises and other places that sold processed meat and other foods packed with cholesterol. This was the food that was responsible for destroying the health of so many people. He thought about his grandfather's poor health. He didn't want that for himself, his family, or his friends.

Working at the restaurant was starting to take a toll on Jayden. Although he had gotten used to going to work and performing his job duties and he liked his coworkers and looked forward to seeing them every day (and sometimes Tristan and his other friends would even stop by), Jayden was starting to see his job as a burden. It was a burden to his community because the restaurant was serving unhealthy food to his peers and elders, causing generation after generation to fall ill. And it was a burden to animals because they were being mass-produced and slaughtered by the millions.

Felipe came into the preparation area where Jayden was working. He wanted to know why the

chicken preparation had slowed down. "Jay, we gotta speed it up! You're falling behind, kid. This isn't like you." Felipe sounded frustrated.

As he was battering the chicken, Jayden replied, "Well, it's not easy for me to come here and do this anymore."

Felipe looked confused. "What are you talking about? We have a line of hungry customers out there!"

"Do you even care that these chickens were once innocent living creatures?" Jayden asked while continuing to batter the chicken parts.

"Is this more of that animal rights stuff?" Felipe responded angrily. "I don't want to hear any more of that nonsense about animals! Get your head in the game. We're running low on battered chicken!"

Jayden turned to Felipe and said quietly, "I'm outta here." He took off his apron and crossed over to the sink to wash his hands.

Felipe was furious! "Are you seriously doing this right now?!" He stood with his hands on his hips looking at Jayden in disbelief. "We need to get this chicken out now! Customers are waiting!" he yelled.

Jayden turned away from the sink and looked Felipe in the eye. "Everything about this is wrong. It's a shame you can't see it because you're blinded by the promise of getting promoted. We're helping people destroy their own health with this food. I can't do it anymore! Your promotion to manager is going to come at the cost of poisoning your own community!"

Felipe stood there in disbelief, trying to understand what had just happened. Jayden didn't say another word. He just turned and walked out the delivery door without looking back.

Chapter Nine

Liberation Begins

Manhattan, N.Y.
August 20, 12:35 p.m.

Jayden traveled by train to get to the Upper East Side of Manhattan, where he was applying for a new job working in a mailroom. He had found the job online and was going in for an interview. He knew he had to work, and he didn't want to disappoint his mother. Working in food service was out of the question after what he had learned about animal agriculture and how the food he was preparing was affecting the long-term health of others.

Walking along Fifth Avenue, he took notice of the clothing boutiques and their expensive garments. All the famous designers' store windows were clean and eye-catching, some with mannequins in summer-themed clothing. Some displayed shoes and handbags made out of alligator, ostrich, and other exotic animal skins. Shaking his head in disgust, he wondered how a whole fashion industry could be so inconsiderate of animals and demonstrate a total disregard for their lives just to make clothing.

A few blocks from his destination, Jayden saw a large crowd ahead in front of Belle & Co., a famous haute couture brand worn by top celebrities and athletes. There were a few dozen people standing in front of the store holding signs advocating for animal rights. They were chanting along with a woman holding a megaphone. She was shouting, "Shut them down!" and "There's no excuse for animal abuse!" and the protesters were backing her up.

Jayden was curious, so he inched closer and closer to the crowd until he looked like he was with them. "What's going on here?" he asked one of the protesters.

The man turned to Jayden and said, "We're protesting Belle & Co. for their sale of exotic animal skins and fur!" Jayden was awe-struck.

He had watched videos of protests on WebVideos, but he had never attended one in person. He had 30 minutes before he was to be interviewed for the mailroom position, so he decided to stick around and watch the protest. People walking by on the street stopped for a few seconds to see what was happening. They took pictures with their phones then continued moving along. Some people laughed at the protesters, mocking them for "protesting fashion" as one bystander put it.

"They're protesting the use of *innocent animals* for fashion!" Jayden snapped at the bystander. "These animals should be living their lives free from our interference!" He stared angrily at the bystander who had made the insensitive comment.

"You guys should be protesting more serious issues than this!" the bystander sneered at Jayden. "There's homelessness and other things more important than animals!"

"Yeah, what are you doing about those issues?" Jayden shot back. The man fell silent, not knowing what to say. "You criticize people for trying to make a change, but what are you doing about homelessness?" Jayden asked him again. "What are you doing for anybody?" The man rolled his eyes dismissively at Jayden before he and his friends walked away.

The protester Jayden had been speaking to saw what happened between him and the rude bystander. "You seem to care about animals a lot!" the protester said admiringly. "You speak with so much passion and conviction!"

Jayden nodded. "Yeah, it isn't fair. These animals are taken out of their habitat and made into clothing. I agree with what you guys are doing."

"My name is DJ. That's great that you care about animals!"

Jayden shook DJ's hand and introduced himself. "I've never seen people protesting for animal rights before. It's really inspiring."

"Well you're always welcome to join us, Jayden. We're with an organization called SAFE. It stands for 'Saving Animals From Everyone.'

Animals need as many voices defending them as possible."

"I'm familiar with the LIFE movement," Jayden told him. "Their videos opened my eyes and changed my perspective on animals, for sure!"

"Yes, they are an amazing group of people!" DJ exclaimed, "LIFE videos are really reaching people. We here at SAFE are trying to do the same thing."

Jayden liked the idea of being an activist. Ever since going vegan, he wanted to advocate for animals and people's health. "That sounds great!" he replied. "I'd like to stay here longer, but I have an important job interview to get to right now."

DJ gave Jayden his phone number. "Next weekend, we're going to protest the grand opening of Baby Fresh in Downtown Manhattan. They're a cosmetics brand notorious for testing their skin-care products on animals, and it has to stop!"

"Thanks, DJ! I'll give you a call." Jayden headed off to his job interview.

"I hope to see you there, Jayden!" yelled DJ over the loud protesters. "Animals need your voice!"

Chapter Ten

My Friend Is a Stranger

Brownsville, Brooklyn, N.Y.
August 26, 12:30 p.m.

Jayden was at home blending a smoothie and relaxing when Tristan texted him to say he was coming over. A few minutes went by, and there was a knock on the door. Jayden let Tristan in, along with another friend named Rell. "Jay, I haven't seen you in a while! You must be working hard, bro!" Tristan boomed.

The boys laughed and went to Jayden's bedroom to hang out. Tristan started telling Jayden about all the fun he'd been having, traveling to different cities in the Tri-State Area, meeting girls, and enjoying different beaches, parties, and amusement parks. "Yo, Jay, tell your job to give you a vacation from cooking chicken all summer to hang out with ya boy!" Tristan said jokingly. "They working you too hard, bro!"

Tristan and Rell laughed. But Jayden wasn't laughing. "I quit that job, Tris."

Tristan looked at him in shock. "Bro, you serious? Does your mom know?"

Jayden shook his head and sighed. "No, I'm waiting to hear back about this mailroom job in Manhattan."

Rell chimed in and asked, "Why'd you quit? You was makin' money. You could buy all the fly gear you wanted, *and* they was giving you free meals, kid. What's up?"

Jayden paused for a moment. He looked at his two friends and asked, "Do you guys ever give any thought to how many animals are slaughtered for food on a daily basis?" Tristan and Rell looked at each other and burst out laughing.

"Jay, are you OK, bro?" asked Rell. "What does that have to do with work?"

Jayden looked at Rell. "That job opened my eyes to how desensitized we are as a community to the suffering of animals and to our own health. We're killing millions of animals each day just to enjoy the way they taste. But eating them is what's making our community sick!" he exclaimed passionately.

Tristan started to realize how serious Jayden was. "Jayden I hear what you're saying, but you eat meat, too, and I know how much you love the chicken at Roasters."

Jayden looked at his best friend and said thoughtfully, "I used to. I couldn't keep working there knowing I was contributing to animal suffering and people's health issues."

Rell was impatient. "Jay, it's not like you're killing the animals yourself. Plus, it's OK to eat them. Animals don't know what's going on. God put them here for us to eat, bro! Cycle of life!"

"It's really a cycle of death!" Jayden exclaimed. "These animals have a soul, and we're eating them, only to end up with heart disease, high blood pressure, and cancer as a result. Don't you see how this food is destroying the health of our neighbors?" He felt frustrated. "Everything that kills us is within arms' reach! Fried chicken,

processed burgers, liquor stores ... where are the farmers' markets? Where are the health food stores, like they have in other neighborhoods with higher tax brackets? These food deserts are making us sick! They give us high blood pressure, heart disease, and cancer. We're getting sick and dying young! We have to stop eating these innocent animals and be more responsible for our own health!"

Tristan's eyes widened as Jayden was talking. "Bro, you are so right! I never looked at things that way before!"

"I don't eat meat or dairy anymore, Rell. I'm vegan for animals and for my health," Jayden explained. "We can't afford to keep eating meat. We have to eat more plant-based foods."

Tristan looked at Jayden appreciatively and said, "That's what's up, bro. I like how you're always seeing things from a different perspective."

But Rell still couldn't believe it. "What are you talking about? What's a vegan?" he asked irritably. "That sounds like some kind of hippie baloney!"

"It means I don't eat animal products or wear animal skin. We have to change the way we treat animals, Rell."

Rell rolled his eyes and pointed to Jayden's sneaker collection. "So that means you're not going to wear Air Wavy's anymore?" he asked sarcastically. You know what they're made of, right? Leather and suede. Also, those are your favorite kicks! I can't remember the last time I saw you without a pair on your feet!"

"No, Rell—no more Wavy's, no more leather coats, and no more leather belts. I'm getting rid of everything made out of animal skin and donating it. It's torture and it's shameful."

Rell looked at him in shock. He couldn't believe what he was hearing. "You sound like you're in a cult or something, bro!"

Tristan had been listening to the conversation between his two friends. "I mean Jayden is making a lot of sense," he said. "It just seems like it's all senseless killing, I guess."

"Man, both of y'all are bugging!" Rell responded indignantly. "This is crazy! Yo, I'm out. Tristan, you want to go get a bite to eat? Jayden's bugging right now!" He stood up to leave.

Tristan looked down at the floor and didn't respond. Rell waved his hand dismissively and

headed toward the door. "I'm out! All this talk about food is making me hungry. I'm going to

Roasters to get some greasy FRIED CHICKEN!"
he slammed the door on his way out.

Tristan looked at Jayden. "You know, I never
thought about things the way you described it.
You've definitely given me a lot to think about."

Chapter Eleven

The Power of the People

Downtown Manhattan, N.Y.
August 28, 1:02 p.m.

Just as promised, Jayden met up with DJ and a few other members of SAFE. He was excited to take part in a protest for animal rights. Since working at the restaurant and learning about factory farming and the different ways animals are mistreated and killed, he had been feeling betrayed by society and all that he had been taught concerning animals. He now felt the need to inform others about the injustices animals face and the negative impact that has on society.

DJ was excited to see Jayden. "I'm so glad you made it!" he said and gave him a hug. "Let me introduce you to some amazing friends and activists!" DJ directed him toward a group of protesters. Jayden shook hands with a few people as DJ introduced him.

He shook one woman's hand and remarked, "I remember you. You were leading a protest last week on Fifth Avenue."

She smiled. "Yes, I'm Lisa. I'm one of SAFE's organizers."

"Well it's really nice to meet you!" Jayden responded. "What you do is truly inspiring." Jayden met the other protesters, who were from different ethnic backgrounds and professions. Teachers, lawyers, construction workers, and all different types of people were there doing their part to speak up for animals.

Lisa was a small-business owner. She had a vegan bakery in the Lower East Side of Manhattan called Sweetie Pie Bakery. "So, Jayden, what made you decide to go vegan? You must have a passion for animal rights if you're here with us today!"

"It wasn't until I worked at New Orleans Roasters that I realized that animals are mass-produced so businesses can profit off them. These animals are forced to live in horrific conditions before they're killed just so people can enjoy their flesh for a 10-minute meal. I didn't want to be a part of their suffering anymore, so I quit."

Lisa smiled. "That's truly brave and amazing. I'm so glad you're here speaking up for animal liberation with us! Did you find another job yet?"

"I'm waiting for a call back to work in a mail room, but it's been a week. I'm still looking for a job to save money to buy books for college next month," he explained.

"I own a small bakery on the Lower East Side and I can use some help if you're interested," Lisa said. Jayden liked the idea and decided to take her up on her offer.

After chatting a bit, everyone got ready for the Baby Fresh protest. Once the doors opened for business, the protesters focused on educating potential customers about the animal testing involved in Baby Fresh products. Jayden stood with DJ, Lisa, and other protesters holding signs that read, "Boycott Baby Fresh," "Baby Fresh Tests on Animals," "Animals Are Not Lab Tools," and "Go Vegan for Animals!"

There were no less than thirty protesters standing in front of Baby Fresh, vociferously advocating for the animals used for testing. Jayden could tell that the demo was having an effect! He watched as people thought twice about shopping in the store after learning about the company's cruel practices. He watched as activists reached out to passersby, raising their awareness of the cruelty involved in animal testing and explaining that supporting products that have been tested on animals is supporting torture.

But some customers were unfazed and went into the store anyway. Jayden realized that not everyone cared about animals, but he also realized that there were people still in the dark about animal cruelty and that spreading information was vital. In that moment, he knew he wanted to spread awareness in his own neighborhood. He realized that he felt very passionately about saving the lives of animals and preserving human health.

After the protest was over, DJ, Lisa, Jayden, and a few others decided to go eat at a well-known vegan restaurant not far from Baby Fresh, called Plantastic Eatery. It had a mouth-watering menu with an assortment of dishes, all vegan.

"Jayden, the tacos here are the best!" DJ advised. "SAFE members usually come here after marches and protests." The group ordered then talked and discussed upcoming events as they ate. Lisa spoke with Jayden about working at the bakery. They agreed on a start date and time. Jayden was excited to have taken part in his first protest and also to have landed a job with an ethical vegan business. What a great day it had been!

Chapter Twelve

The Life You Save

New Jersey
September 4, 12:35 p.m.

SAFE was planning a bus trip to visit an animal sanctuary in New Jersey called Better Haven Animal Sanctuary. Jayden signed up to attend the trip and asked Tristan to go, too. Since the two hadn't had a chance to hang out and enjoy each other's company all summer, Jayden thought they could catch up while visiting the sanctuary and seeing the rescued animals. "Thanks for coming, Tris. I know we haven't really had much time to hang out this summer."

Tristan playfully put Jayden in a headlock. "No doubt, Jay, you my boy!" he said gleefully. "I know how much this vegan stuff means to you. Let's go make some animal friends!"

The boys, along with the other SAFE members, were greeted at the sanctuary by the farm owners and given safety instructions, rules, and regulations to follow during their visit. Then it was time to take the tour. The boys were amazed at the animals. Being from the city, they had never seen farmed animals up close and personal.

They were in awe of the size of the cows and how gentle they were.

They watched the turkeys strut around and enjoy the companionship of the people who came to visit them. They laughed at the playful piglets tumbling over each other. Dozens of other rescued animals occupied every acre of the farm's land. Sheep, lambs, rabbits, goats, and so many more animals called Better Haven Sanctuary home.

DJ, Lisa, and a few other SAFE members were taking selfies with the animals and petting them. Jayden and Tristan left the group to go see the chickens, since they had been crucial to Jayden's decision to go vegan. They stopped at the fenced-off area where dozens of rescued chickens and hens were mingling. Jayden gazed at them with a feeling of sadness and shame.

"Tristan, do you realize that these animals were rescued from us? People who find enjoyment in eating them?" he said somberly. "All these chickens would have ended up as part of a meal if they hadn't been rescued."

Tristan nodded. He stuck his hand out, and the birds came over to greet him and let him pet them and rub their feathers. "You know what, Jay? I see what you're talking about. I look into these animals' eyes, and I see a soul. They trust us so much, and we betray them. The cows, pigs—all of them—they trust us, and we pay back their loyalty by killing them."

Jayden reached out to touch the hens and murmured sadly, "You're right. We don't deserve their trust."

Tristan felt a pang of regret. "Bro, I feel you on this vegan stuff. I can't eat meat anymore after looking these animals in the eye, man." The boys spent a few more minutes visiting the chickens before reuniting with the rest of the group. After a few more hours at the sanctuary, everyone got back on the bus to head back to New York.

Tristan left with a new perspective on animals and Jayden with a passion to inform others in his community about the importance of empathy for all.

Chapter Thirteen

A Different World

Lower East Side, Manhattan, N.Y.
September 14, 3:30 p.m.

Jayden was wrapping up his day at the Sweetie Pie bakery. He had started at 7 a.m., and his shift was almost done. He had been there for a week, and he loved it! He was learning how to bake and design cakes, all while enjoying interacting with the customers and meeting other vegans who were just as passionate about animal rights as he was. He met a young man named Ahmed who came to the bakery often for coffee and some muffins.

Ahmed ran a small business called Kompassion Kicks. His store sold sneakers, baseball caps, and seasonal garments that were all ethical and fair trade items. His main products were sneakers! The brands of sneakers that Ahmed sold were made out of hemp, canvas, or even apple or pineapple leather. Everything was vegan and ethically sourced. Ahmed encouraged Jayden to stop by. "Come and check us out, Jayden! We're two blocks down on Prince Street near the train station."

"Cool! I definitely will!" Jayden responded with a big grin. Only two months ago, Jayden didn't even know what a vegan was, and now he was in the middle of a world that focused on saving animals and living life cruelty-free. What he liked about being in the Lower East Side of the city was that most of the businesses were vegan. The restaurants, clothing stores, and small shops that sold skin care products didn't exploit animals to make a profit. There were markets that sold fresh, organic fruits and vegetables. One market in particular made fresh juices and smoothies that Jayden liked to drink on his lunch break. He started to shed those unhealthy pounds that he had gained from working at Roasters and eating fried chicken every night.

But what bothered him was that his own neighborhood was still a food desert. The residents simply bought what was available to them. The majority of the people didn't prioritize eating healthfully because it was too expensive and they could only access fresh fruits and vegetables by traveling to other neighborhoods, which for many, was too difficult. Jayden thought that should change.

He knew of the upcoming grand opening of a New Orleans Roasters in his neighborhood and wanted to do something to inform the residents of his neighborhood about the dangers of eating high-cholesterol, animal-based foods and what happens to the millions of animals who are slaughtered to make it.

"Hey, Lisa," Jayden said. "New Orleans Roasters is going to open another restaurant. This time in my neighborhood."

"This is going to be the 21st Roasters in Brooklyn alone," Lisa complained, giving Jayden her undivided attention. "What do you have in mind?"

"I want to protest the opening of that restaurant! The more of these restaurants that open up, the higher the demand will be for these unhealthy foods and for animals to be slaughtered.

My neighborhood can't afford to see any more fast-food places open up. We need vegetable markets and health food stores. Kids are suffering from childhood obesity, and the elderly are suffering from high blood pressure and even heart disease, and it's all because most of the food available in the neighborhood is unhealthy!"

Lisa nodded. "We can definitely make our voices heard. Let me know the date of the grand opening, so I can post it on MediaPage." She planned to gather support from SAFE members to help with Jayden's protest. She saw his passion for saving animals and preserving people's health and wanted to help him.

Chapter Fourteen

Family Matters

Brownsville, Brooklyn, N.Y.
September 20, 5 p.m.

Jayden was home making smoothies for himself and Tara. He combined bananas, strawberries, oats, and cashew milk in the blender, making sure he added extra strawberries for his sister, to make it a bit sweeter. He took the smoothies and went to sit on the couch with her to watch her favorite TV shows. She took a sip of her smoothie and raved, "This is soooo good!"

Jayden smiled. "I'm glad you like it. I'll make them for you whenever you want." They sat together watching cartoons. Hearing her kids laughing in the living room, Ms. Young came in from the back of the apartment. Tara looked up and asked, "Mommy, do you want some of my smoothie? Jayden made it, and it's so good!"

Ms. Young smiled at Tara. "Maybe later, sweetie. I have to talk to your brother, OK?"

Jayden looked at his mother and could see she had some concerns. "Everything OK, Ma?" he asked. He knew something was wrong, so he got up to go talk with her in her bedroom. "I'll be right back, Tara."

Ms. Young sat on the edge of her bed, and Jayden leaned against the wall beside the dresser. "When were you going to tell me you quit your job?"

Jayden shrugged his shoulders. "I don't know, Ma. I didn't want you to get upset with me or anything," he replied, suddenly feeling guilty. "But I found a new job working in the city at a bakery."

"Why did you quit Roasters?" she asked. "I'm glad you're working somewhere else, but you should never quit a job without giving them proper notice."

Jayden sat down on the bed next to his mother. "You're right. You taught me better than that. But I couldn't stand another second in that place, knowing I was contributing to people's illnesses. Ma, you taught me to seek the truth and stand up for what I believe in, so that's what I'm doing."

Ms. Young smiled and patted her son's face. "You know, you are wise beyond your 17 years." Then she closed her eyes for a moment and sighed. "I also wanted to tell you that I went to see my doctor a few days ago. She put me on medication for high blood pressure and warned that I'm running the risk of getting type 2 diabetes."

Jayden felt a wave of panic, but before he could say anything, his mother assured him that she would be OK. "Don't worry about me, Jay. I'm going to take good care of myself and your sister. The doctor told me to stay away from certain foods, and I have to say, you were right, baby. The foods we are eating are doing more harm than good. There're going to be some changes around here. I've been doing a little research on this plant-based diet, and I'd like to try it out. The doctor told me to stay away from red and processed meat."

Jayden smiled. "Don't worry, Ma. I'm going to take care of you." He gave his mother a hug and then offered to make her a smoothie.

"I would love to try one, Jay!" She smiled with appreciation as they returned to the living room. They talked a bit more about the benefits of going vegan. Jayden told his mother all about the new job and the remarkable friendships he had made over the summer. He also told her about the upcoming protest he was involved in. She expressed concern for his safety, but Jayden assured her he would be fine.

"It's a peaceful protest, Ma. We have to let big businesses like Roasters know they can't keep making money in our neighborhood while destroying our health and sacrificing innocent animals along the way!"

Chapter Fifteen

The Art of Liberation

Brownsville, Brooklyn, N.Y.
September 24, 1:30 p.m.

The grand opening of New Orleans Roasters in Brownsville was underway. There were red-white-and-blue banners adorning the entrance to the store and a large 7-foot sign right outside promoting the grand opening sale: "BUY TWO BUCKETS OF FRIED OR ROTISSERIE CHICKEN AND GET THREE SIDE DISHES FREE!"

The store clearly expected to have a successful grand opening. Jayden, DJ, Lisa, and about a dozen other activists from SAFE were standing to the side of the entrance, holding signs that read: "Roasters Kills Chickens," "Stop Paying for Animal Cruelty," and "More Farmers' Markets, Less Fried Chicken."

Some activists were handing out leaflets with information about factory farming and how chickens are treated on these farms to potential Roasters customers. They also handed out leaflets with easy vegan recipes. Lisa and Jayden had taken the day off from the bakery to participate in the protest.

Tristan showed up as well to support his best friend. "You really opened my eyes, Jay. I just wanna say I got your back, bro!"

Jayden gave him a hug and thanked him. The SAFE members were out in front of the restaurant for a few hours and encountered people from the neighborhood who weren't willing to listen to what they were saying. Most just ignored the protesters and went inside to eat. People stood on the sidewalk with their phones, posting videos online of what was happening, some even making fun of the protesters.

One bystander, a man in his late thirties, approached Jayden to ask him what the protest was all about. "Yo, kid! Why y'all out here harassing people about buying chicken?"

"We're here to bring awareness to our community about the problems with fast-food restaurants in the neighborhood."

"What problem? Ya'll don't have the right to tell people what they can eat. It's a free country!" Jayden explained, "Franchises like New Orleans Roasters target and exploit poor urban communities. Their food contributes to childhood obesity, high blood pressure in young adults, and heart disease in the elderly, and their food can potentially cause cancer as well."

Jayden had the man's attention now. "You serious, kid? These restaurants are serving us food that could give us cancer?" He looked shocked.

"Take a look around you. We all know somebody who is suffering from one of the illnesses I just mentioned." He raised his voice. "And these franchises are also cruel to animals. Chickens live in extremely cramped conditions and are treated very badly. They're fed an unnatural diet and antibiotics to make them grow more quickly so restaurants like this one can make more money. Then we consume these animals, and that's killing us!" The more Jayden talked, the more people gathered around to listen.

"Innocent animals are being forcibly bred and dosed with antibiotics and other chemicals and then killed by the millions every day and served to us! People don't consider the lives of these animals because we're taught that their whole purpose is to die and become nothing more than a two-piece meal!" he continued passionately. More people started gathering and taking in Jayden's words. "All of these restaurants in our neighborhood are serving us carcinogenic, processed animal flesh. And now *another* fried chicken restaurant? We have to be more accountable for our own health! Where are the farmers' markets and health food stores in our neighborhood?"

Nobody listening could answer the question, but people were shaking their heads and agreeing with Jayden. "Our people's health is important! Animals' lives are important! Our council members, mayor, and all these officials we elect to office must know that we can't afford any more fast-food restaurants in our neighborhoods. We elect these officials because we trust them to do what's best for the people in the community, and they're putting corporate profit over the people! We need healthier food options, not food that's shortening our life expectancy and the lives of animals!" Some of the bystanders started clapping. Jayden felt empowered.

The man Jayden had originally been speaking to smiled and extended his hand to Jayden. Jayden shook the man's hand and smiled back. "Little brother, I never heard nobody talk like that before," he said. "I was going to go in there and get some chicken for dinner, but you gave me something else to think about now." Other people nodded their heads in agreement.

Now more people were turning away from the restaurant. This caught the attention of the restaurant manager, who made his way outside to confront the protesters. "Jayden, what are you doing?!" he yelled. It was Felipe. He had recently been promoted to manager of the new restaurant, and he was furious.

"You're driving away my customers with your animal rights nonsense!"

The man Jayden had been talking to fired back at Felipe, "Let the young brother talk! He's not bothering anybody!"

Felipe, standing in the entrance to the restaurant shot back, "Jayden, you've got one minute to clear out of here before I call the cops!"

"This is a peaceful protest, and we're not breaking any laws, sir," Lisa informed Felipe. "We have every right to be here." Felipe was furious and stormed back inside, cursing. Jayden gave Lisa a hug and thanked her for everything she had done for him.

People approached Jayden to shake his hand and take selfies with him. The older man Jayden had been talking to declared, "You're a positive young man. This community needs young men like you fighting for it!" Jayden smiled and thanked him as he walked away.

Tristan turned to Jayden and told him how proud he was to have him for a friend. "That man is right, Jay. You gave a lot of people here something to think about today. I never thought about how much harm is done to animals until I heard you say it, and I never gave any thought to how unhealthfully we eat until I heard *you* say it. Everybody who heard you today is going to remember what you said. You're saving lives, bro!" Tristan playfully jabbed Jayden on the shoulder.

They lingered a bit longer, talking to the people in the neighborhood about the benefits of a vegan lifestyle.

Chapter Sixteen

Changing Course

Manhattan, N.Y.
September 30, 6:15 p.m.

Jayden ended his shift at Sweetie Pie bakery and was on his way to his first class at college. He kept his job with Lisa during the morning and dedicated his weeknights to attending classes.

He remembered the words of the older man at the protest. They echoed in his head: "This community needs young men like you fighting for it." He decided to switch his college major to political science. While participating in activism on the streets was effective, he knew the best way to change the system was from the inside. If he really wanted to help the animal rights cause and advocate for healthier foods in poor communities, he would have to make it a political fight. "This community needs young men like you fighting for it." Those words stayed with him. He knew his community needed an advocate. He knew animals did, too.

Epilogue
Liberation for Life

Over the next 10 years, Jayden graduated from college with a degree in political science and also became a certified nutritionist. He ran for councilmember of his district and won, becoming one of the youngest council members in Brooklyn. He started to push for healthier vegan alternatives in schools in his district as well as citywide. He pushed for farmers' markets in the inner cities so families would have access to fresh fruits and vegetables daily.

His passion was still animal rights, and he remained very active in the animal liberation movement. He pushed hard to ban the sale of exotic skins and fur in New York as well as to mandate that all nonvegan restaurants include vegan options on their menus.

Jayden went on to become the mayor of New York City in 2030. He knew the fight for animal liberation would never be easy, but he gladly accepted the responsibility of trying to make his city and the world a better place for all sentient beings. His motto was "Liberate your mind. Liberate animals. Liberate humanity."

Stewart Mitchell is a father, author, poet and an advocate for human and animal rights. He is from Brooklyn, New York.
Facebook: Stewart Mitchell
Instagram: @vigilante_vegan
email: stewartmitchell1978@gmail.com

VOICE4CHANGE LLC

Original publication 2019